MEET THE GRUBBLERS

Written by
Sarah Louise

Illustrated by
Amy Ashworth

D1407355

SilverWood

Published in 2021 by SilverWood Books

SilverWood Books Ltd
14 Small Street, Bristol, BS1 1DE, United Kingdom
www.silverwoodbooks.co.uk

ISBN 978-1-80042-158-5 (paperback)

British Library Cataloguing in Publication Data
A CIP catalogue record for this book is
available from the British Library

Page design and typesetting by SilverWood Books

SARAH LOUISE has always had a talent for connecting with and inspiring children of all ages. Having worked in schools for twenty-five years, Sarah has now expanded her educational expertise into being an author. She hopes to provide exciting and page-turning stories that capture the minds of the younger generation of today.

Sarah has three adult children of her own, a beautiful granddaughter and a much-loved cockapoo. She resides in the county of Wiltshire.

Find out more at sarahlouisenovels.com

For Bonnie, love you always.

Chapter 1

Closing down her iPad and falling back against the softness of her pillow, Emily felt an overwhelming sense of sadness. She missed her friends and her dad. Online chats no longer held the excitement that they did at the start of the pandemic. With a sigh, she glanced up to see the last shred of daylight fight through the curtains. She marvelled at just how still it was. Unusually, there were no shadows or movements that Emily could see. Feeling brave, she crept out of bed and carefully tiptoed towards the rose-patterned curtains. Cautiously drawing them back, she stared in wonder at the scene before her. Instead of the row upon row of identical houses that usually met her gaze, there were trees, lots of trees glowing with the colours of autumn. The late evening light had been replaced by the darkening autumnal sky. The noises she had heard she now recognised as being the sounds of the wind rustling crisp leaves as they floated to the ground. Emily, head in hands as she leant on her windowsill, was quite bewildered by what she could see.

Suddenly, her gaze fell upon a figure, a lonely figure sitting against one of the trees, deep in thought with chin resting on her knees. Emily found herself quite drawn to this person. As Emily gazed, the young girl lifted her head and gazed back, giving Emily the opportunity to appreciate what she saw. The girl had long, dark, unkempt hair, was slight of build and had a perfect snow-white complexion. As the girl's emerald-green eyes smiled warmly, Emily felt a strange sensation come over her. She felt dizzy, sick even. Grabbing the windowsill, she held the little girl's gaze.

Gradually, the windowsill slipped from her grasp. Her feet felt light and airy. Emily could no longer feel the comfort of her soft bedroom carpet beneath her feet. A cold, damp sensation encircled her toes as she found herself at the top of a stone staircase. Looking around, she was surprised to find no sign of her bedroom, the bookcase or her cuddly toys. All alone, she stood at the top of the stairs.

"Come on, come on," a voice shouted from the bottom of the stairs. "I've been waiting ages for you."

Warily, Emily looked down to see the little girl had moved from the foot of the tree to the foot of the stairs. Emily felt drawn to the voice and began to make her way slowly towards the girl. Each step was cold underfoot and Emily wished she had put slippers on. As she reached the bottom step, her arm was roughly grabbed and pulled. Emily felt her heart start to race; her parents were quite clear that she should have no physical contact with anyone during these difficult times. Reluctantly, she followed her arm until she found herself under the tree where she had first spotted the little girl.

"Sorry about that, but I couldn't risk us being seen. They don't like strangers, you know," said the girl.

Emily stared at the young girl in front of her. It was unnerving, like looking in a mirror. Standing well back, Emily stammered, "Who... who...who doesn't like strangers?"

"Mr and Mrs White," the girl replied. "They live in the big house over there."

Emily looked to where the girl was pointing only to see that her ordinary family home had been replaced by a sinister-looking mansion. Large iron gates were supported by an imposing wall, which encircled the whole house.

"How do you do? My name is Lucy," said the little girl, extending her hand for Emily to shake.

A bemused Emily was very concerned as to what had happened to her home and her family who a short time ago were inside watching television. Ignoring the girl's proffered hand, she announced, "I'm Emily."

"I know that! You look freezing. Come on, let's get home and warm you up."

Emily *was* cold, particularly her feet. The nightdress she was wearing was a thin summer one with a picture of a contented cat on the front, and the chill evening air was penetrating the flimsy material. She began to shiver.

Lucy was skipping off through the trees whilst Emily, having to be wary of where she stood, struggled to keep up. Keeping her eyes rooted to the ground, Emily marvelled at the soft mossy feeling underfoot, being careful not to stand on sharp twigs, which littered the ground like shards of glass. Eventually, they came to a road with small cottages either side. As Emily cautiously followed Lucy, she had a strange feeling that she had been here before. Each cottage was different. Some were rather dilapidated and in need of repair. Others looked homely with smoke rising from the chimneys, assuring visitors of a warm and friendly welcome.

A large wooden cart passed slowly by, pulled by a rather old and weary-looking horse. "Hurry along now, Miss Lucy," called out the elderly gentleman who was driving the cart. "Your ma will be worrying about you."

"I'm hurrying. I'm hurrying," Lucy shouted back, as she skipped along the dirt track of a road.

"Who is that?" enquired Emily as she dodged yet another sharp stone.

"Mr Rogers – he delivers our coal. My ma is always moaning to him about how often I disappear... We're here now!"

They had arrived at a small welcoming cottage, the door of which opened straight onto the road. Lucy banged her fist hard on the black wooden door several times before it was opened by a small, cross-looking lady wearing the most unusual spectacles. Emily noticed that the glass in the spectacles was as thick as the bottom of the wine bottles carefully stacked in her father's wine rack. They sat on the lady's nose in a most peculiar way.

"Where have you been? Where have you been?" shrieked the woman.

"I had to wait for Emily, Ma. She wouldn't come straight away. We need her help to get Ada back!"

Following Lucy down a short narrow passageway, ensuring that she kept a safe distance apart, Emily found herself in a snug kitchen with a low-beamed ceiling and rough, whitewashed walls. In the centre of the room was a small, well-scrubbed wooden table surrounded by four rickety chairs. In one corner of the room, a large open cupboard stood floor to ceiling, cluttered with an assortment of pots and pans. Amongst the mayhem, the solemn expression of Queen Victoria in her later years stared blankly towards the centre of the room. Emily had enjoyed the Year 4 topic on the Victorians, one of the many things that had been cut short when the pandemic struck. She really enjoyed history; it made her think about how what happens in the past affects the future. She had recently been reading about the Spanish flu pandemic of 1918 and how people coped in such unique circumstances. She would often find herself snuggled under the warmth of her duvet comparing then to today.

As Lucy's mum tutted and fussed around her daughter, Emily's thoughts turned to her aching feet and Lucy's words. Ada? Who was Ada?

"Feet in the bowl, dear. Hurry now, feet in the bowl. The water won't stay warm for long!"

The shrill voice made Emily jump to attention as she squeezed her tired feet into a very small bowl.

Chapter 2

Everything was happening too quickly. It seemed no time at all since Emily had been lying in her own bed, deep in thought, trying to make sense of the strange situation the world found itself in.

As these memories crowded her mind, tears slowly trickled down her face. Refusing the help of the kind, bespectacled lady, Emily caressed her tender feet with a yearning desire for the comforting feel of her own mother's hands. So many unanswered questions swirled around in her head. She had no idea where she was and why she was there.

Suddenly, a loud crash came from the back garden followed by another and another. Rubbing at her steam-covered glasses, Lucy's mother sighed. "Oh, goodness! Not again, not again..."

She bustled out of the small back door, quickly followed by Lucy. Emily sat still, feet squashed into the bowl as the water started to turn really quite cold. After a short while, Lucy returned.

"Ma's really mad. They've knocked over the water butt again and it was nearly full!"

"Who's 'they'?" asked a bewildered Emily.

"Grubblers, of course…"

"Grubblers?"

Lucy beckoned her towards the back door. Emily dried her feet with the small towel provided and peered through the door. Lucy's mother was shrieking across the neat garden at what looked like four little old men cartwheeling and laughing at her. One of them spotted Emily and stuck out a very long, warty tongue in her direction.

Emily jumped as she heard the front door slam shut and a voice boom through the house.

"No one to greet me then?"

At this, a large jolly-looking man appeared in the doorway, his round face breaking out into a broad smile as he spotted Emily.

"Ah! This must be the little one who is going to help get our Ada back."

Remembering the need to keep her distance, Emily introduced herself. "Good afternoon, sir. My name is Emily."

"Good afternoon, young Emily. Jack Weaver, pleased to meet you."

Emily stared intently at Jack. He really was a jolly-looking man. She decided that he reminded her very much of Father Christmas. Not that she had ever met Father Christmas in person, but if she did, she was sure he would be just like Jack.

"Mrs Weaver! Mrs Weaver!" Jack was bellowing as he swung around the kitchen searching for his wife. His eyes settled on a rather delicious-looking fruit cake, which had pride of place on the kitchen table.

"She's in the garden," said a rather puzzled Emily.

She decided Jack probably hadn't heard her, as he was searching the cutlery drawer for something to cut the cake with. Moments later, his head found its way out of the cutlery drawer. "What's she doing in the garden? Oh no! They're back, aren't they?" He sighed as he disappeared through the back door.

As the rumpus in the garden carried on, Lucy came back in the kitchen and collapsed in front of a bewildered Emily.

"Who's Ada?" Emily asked.

"She's my cousin," said Lucy. "She's lived with us since her parents died."

Before Emily could respond, Lucy continued, explaining how Ada had been watching over Emily like a guardian angel. She

15

knew Emily was unhappy and worried about the pandemic and just wanted to help. "She often sat behind your bedroom curtains, just watching, willing you into an untroubled sleep," she finished.

Emily had often noticed a certain flicker across the curtain or an unexplained shadow, but had been too scared to investigate.

Suddenly, Lucy jumped up and began eyeing the fruit cake still sitting proudly in the middle of the table. She turned to her new-found friend and smiled. "Ada always looks after you. Now it's your turn to help her."

The realisation hit Emily that Lucy must've been waiting for Ada when they met under the tree. Where could the shadow behind the curtain have disappeared to? How on earth was she supposed to find her?

"We must get her back as soon as possible. She has the knack of coping with those rascals." Lucy's mother flopped into the chair opposite Emily with her glasses hanging precariously from her nose. Her hair stuck shiny and wet to her forehead.

"Nowt will be achieved tonight, my dear, and these girls need their beds," sighed a very dishevelled-looking Jack, as he returned from the garden.

As Emily rose from the chair, she caught

a glimpse of the devastation that had been wreaked throughout the garden. Her eyes settled on an upturned water butt, swimming through the tide of water it once held. There was an old water butt in her garden, weathered with age but still functional. Memories of her garden, which had become her safe place for the last few weeks, came flooding through her mind and yet again tears began to fall gently over her cheeks.

"I want to see my mum." The words gasped from her mouth as the tears came faster.

"Oh, my goodness, so you will my dear, once we have Ada back. Come along now both of you, up the wooden hill." Lucy's mum bustled both girls out of the warmth of the kitchen towards the narrow, wooden staircase, which led to Lucy's bedroom.

Lucy's bedroom was small and sparse, just a bed, a table and a battered old chest, which lay at the end of her bed. The old wooden floorboards creaked as the girls made their way towards the bed and sat down. Taking in her surroundings through teary eyes, Emily's gaze fell upon a small portrait of a girl. Wiping away her tears, she carefully touched the picture and strangely felt just a little bit happier. Admiring the beautiful long dark hair and snow-white complexion, Emily just knew that this must be Ada. "She's beautiful," Emily sighed.

As the girls lay – Emily on the cramped bed, Lucy on the hard floor – Emily's thoughts kept turning to the portrait. Lots of questions needed answering. Lucy was obviously waiting for Ada under the tree, yet didn't seem surprised to see her, Emily, appear in front of her. There were striking similarities between the three girls and Emily felt a strange connection to the girl in the portrait. What could have happened to her? How did both girls manage to find their way to her home? How and why did they make their way from the nineteenth to the twenty-first century? Emily's heart began to thump madly against her chest as the realisation hit her that they all thought she could find Ada. How could she possibly meet that challenge?

Chapter 3

Streams of light burst through the thin curtains as Emily began to rouse from a restless night.

"You didn't sleep well, did you?" Lucy yawned.

"No, sorry. Did I keep you awake?"

Lucy shrugged her shoulders. "It's OK. Ada is a terrible sleeper, so I'm used to it."

With that, Lucy disappeared downstairs to join her mother.

As Emily lay staring at the portrait of the lost girl, she felt strangely comforted by the muffled voices she could hear through the old, worn floorboards. Then she heard it: tap, tap, tap at the window. She swung her legs out of the bed and made her way towards the sound. On closer inspection, she found nothing at the window and there appeared to be no one in the garden. Climbing back into bed, she heard the noise again. Returning to the window, Emily decided to open it in order to get a better look. The creaking casement opened, and Emily put her head out. Bang – she was hit full in the face. Jumping backwards, she was hit yet again.

Quickly, she shut the window and as she started to rub the sore feeling in her cheeks, she saw him: a small, elderly-looking man hanging from the tallest tree in Lucy's garden. He reminded Emily of the monkeys at a local safari park. Her dad had often taken her there and she loved the monkeys with their mischievous nature. They would jump on the bonnet of the car, pulling at the windscreen wipers, or just sit on the grass throwing small stones at the moving vehicles. Dad would always complain but deep down she knew he too found them amusing. The thought of her dad made her heart lift and she felt a smile start to spread across her face. She had missed being able to see her dad. Even though the prime minister had said children from split families could stay with either parent, her mum was too worried about Emily catching something to let this happen.

"Off with you! Off with you!" The shrill tones from the garden jolted Emily. As she peered outside, she saw Lucy's mother with a broom in hand chasing the little man out of her garden. Emily started to snigger; the little barefooted man was cartwheeling around the garden until he reached the rickety garden gate. Giving a wink and a toothy grin in Emily's direction, he somersaulted over the gate with ease and disappeared through the maze of hedges that surrounded the quaint cottage.

Later that morning, both girls were getting dressed. Lucy let Emily borrow some clothes, which fitted surprisingly well. Unfortunately, Lucy only had one pair of shoes, but they had found an old pair of Ada's lurking under the stairs. These also fitted surprisingly well. Running her fingers vigorously through her long dark hair, which framed her pale face in a disorderly fashion, Emily's eyes scoured the bedroom looking for anything that could be used as a hair tie. Lucy, sensing her frustration, found a faded blue ribbon lurking at the bottom of the wooden chest.

"I'm sure those grubblers know something. Let's go and see what we can find out."

Emily trotted behind Lucy towards the wooded area at the rear of the cottage. Thoughts of home suddenly rattled through her brain and the sad, helpless feelings from the previous night threatened to return. As they entered the wood, she looked up in wonder at the magnificent canopy of red, orange and brown that shielded the autumn sky.

"Ow! That hurt!" Lucy called out.

Emily jumped as something hit her on the back of her neck. As she rubbed her now stinging neck, something jabbed at the back of her knee, causing her to lose her balance and fall amongst the melange of leaves. She heard yet another yelp from Lucy. What on earth was going on? The girls were being bombarded with small, spiky, acorn-like seeds. As the attack continued, the girls tried to scrabble to safety. Huddled behind a fallen tree, Lucy began rooting around in her pocket.

"Ah ha! Knew it! Remains of a piece of Ma's fruit cake."

"Looks rather squashed!" said Emily, as she peered at the food in her friend's hand.

"I always keep something tasty in my pocket in case I can't get home in time for lunch. Just watch and see what happens."

As the girls crawled beneath a branch of the old oak tree, the small missiles were still raining down around them.

"Mmmmmm...tasty cake," Lucy was shouting. "You really must try some, Emily. My ma sure knows how to bake a cake." Smacking her lips together, Lucy began to smile at Emily. The bombardment of seeds was slowing down and both girls could hear the squeak of movement along the branch above their heads.

Unexpectedly, and before their very eyes, a mop of grey hair swung down from above, rapidly followed by a pair of smoky grey eyes and a bulbous nose.

"I'll have cake," demanded the little old man, as he flipped himself backwards into a standing position in front of the two girls.

He went to snatch the cake, but Lucy was quicker, stuffing the tasty morsel back into her pocket. By this time, a large group of similar little folk had gathered around the girls in a menacing fashion. The words "I'll have cake" echoed around the group as they stared intently at the two young girls.

"You will not have cake!" screeched Lucy. "Not until you have helped us find Ada."

Without warning, the ground beneath them began to rumble. Lucy firmly grasped the opening to her pocket and with her free hand she grabbed an unsuspecting Emily. Emily sprang backwards at the touch on her arm. All around them and above them in the trees little folk were stamping and stomping.

The girls started to tremble, fear taking grip. Sinister faces moved closer and closer.

Boom! The trees shook. Boom! An unearthly silence spread throughout the now still wood. Then the stampede of frightened feet rushing back to where they came from filled the air.

Within moments, the girls were alone, or so they thought…

"Oi! You two shouldn't be hanging around them little blighters. Bad news. Toddle off home." The voice belonged to a rather grumpy-looking man carrying a rather large gun under his arm. Without another word, he mopped his brow and turned to go.

Emily tried hard to suppress a giggle. It may have been nerves, as she did feel quite frightened about all that had just happened, or it could have been the very lacy, delicate hankie he was using to remove the sweat from his face.

Catching Lucy's eye, Emily sensed something wasn't quite right with her friend. Their saviour from the marauding little folk was crashing his way back through the wood mumbling something about pests and thieving as he went.

Lucy slumped back down onto the branch. "They've got Ada. Those from the big house – they've got Ada."

Emily, who had quite forgotten about feeling homesick at this point, looked puzzled. "What do you mean? How do you know?"

"That hankie. My ma embroidered that for Ada. It was a birthday gift."

"Are you sure?" Emily quizzed.

"Quite sure. I recognise the stitching, especially the 'A' in the corner."

Chapter 4

Slowly trudging back through the now still wood, the girls were quiet and thoughtful, until they noticed small circles of smoke wafting in a swirling wave across the woodland carpet. Without uttering a word, they headed towards the spectacle. To their astonishment,  they found a young grubbler lying on his back on a bed of autumn leaves, blowing smoky circles from puffed out cheeks. Both girls stopped and watched as he carefully moved his head to the side, bright blue eyes staring straight into Emily's eyes. The young girl felt rather unnerved but held his gaze. Within seconds, the head slowly returned to its original position and the grubbler carried on with the smoky ritual. An air of uncertainty surrounded the girls as they pondered their next move. Whilst they stood, the smoky rings imperceptibly darkened and spread until the girls were barely visible, entranced by the darkening force surrounding them. Emily felt a hand take her own. Assuming it to be Lucy, she grabbed at the open palm, knowing that she probably shouldn't but yet needing the comfort. Lucy was charging on through the swirling mist and Emily was struggling to keep up with her. Suddenly, the earth was swept from under Emily's feet and she was falling, tumbling downwards at an amazing pace. As she fell, the dense mist gradually began to clear, yet she still couldn't see, it was so dark. Fearfully, she realised she was no longer holding Lucy's hand. What was happening?

With heart racing, Emily scrabbled to her feet. As her eyes grew accustomed to the dark and her nose became accustomed to the musty aroma, she realised she wasn't alone. A loud explosion of gas erupted from the strange little man who was covered in freckles and sported a large ginger beard. The tatty, black bowler hat on his head shook as he roared with laughter at his own rudeness. Emily was far from impressed. She wondered where Lucy was.

Taking in her surroundings, Emily marvelled at the rough, muddy walls, which appeared to be reinforced with roughly chopped branches and twigs. The room itself was sparse with neatly woven willow flooring and a large, gnarled tree root rising up from the middle of the ground. Sitting to the side of this was the strange little man, who on closer inspection looked kinder than the other grubblers Emily had encountered. His clear blue eyes shone with amusement whilst his chubby fingers flicked small insects out of his matted beard (they were attached to what can only be described as morsels of regurgitated food). Although the sight before her was quite disgusting, the young girl marvelled at the army of ant-like creatures disappearing through the willow matting clutching at their prize.

"Well, what has we here then?" he chuckled.

The awkward silence that followed was suddenly broken by a whirlwind of activity and the sparse little room was filled with chatter and a sea of faces. Emily was astounded to see that all the grubblers had beards, and for most of them it was ginger. Cautiously, her eyes panned the room. It was stifling to have so many bodies hemming you in and so many pairs of eyes fixated on you. She began to panic. Should she really be so close to people she didn't know?

"Ouch! That's my toe!" she yelped.

Looking down, Emily's eyes met with a huge grinning face. The straggly beard hung down over a crumpled white shirt and saucer-like green eyes bore into her as the prominent ears began to wiggle.

"You need to help us!"

His voice was much deeper than expected. Puzzled, Emily wasn't too sure how to reply.

A chant then rippled through the room, bouncing repeatedly off the walls. "You need to help us. You need to help us. You need to help us…" It went on and on until Emily felt compelled to cover her ears. The whole room shook, as bullets of mud and shards of twigs rained down on the occupants.

"Enough!" thundered the kind-looking grubbler as he jumped up from his gnarled throne. "Give our guest some space."

As quickly as the room had filled, it emptied.

"Solomon at your service, marm." He chuckled as he doffed his hat in her direction.

Having now removed himself from Emily's feet, the other grubbler took a low bow. "Simpkins, marm. Sorry about your toes!"

Emily could tell he clearly wasn't sorry.

Solomon directed them to sit. Emily tried to make herself as comfortable as she could on the willow flooring, but it wasn't easy. Thoughts of the rotting food and frenzied ants that would be scurrying about beneath her made her squirm.

Folding his arms and allowing short chubby fingers to tap away at his grubby shirt sleeves, the grubbler snorted loudly. "I imagine that you and that bothersome little friend of yours want to get Ada back?"

"I don't really know her, but, yes, Lucy is keen to have her back," replied Emily.

She was very puzzled. What had happened to Lucy?

Chapter 5

Running like the wind, Lucy pushed on through the woods. She wished Emily would hurry and catch her up. The painfully dark sky was gradually retreating until all that was left were wisps of silver and grey curling and dancing amongst the trees. Gasping for breath, she arrived at the grassy clearing that led to her cottage. The wood behind was eerily quiet and a sense of unease overcame her. What had happened to Emily?

As she pushed open the front door, the sweet smell of simmering fruit reached Lucy's nose. She followed the aroma into the kitchen where there was no sign of her mother. Lucy's mouth began to water and the realisation hit her that she was quite hungry. Picking up a nearby wooden spoon, she began to stir the bubbling treat. Feeling rather guilty, Lucy heaped the spoon full of the luxurious mixture. Blowing gently over the scalding mix, her mind began to wander back to the last time she saw Emily.

"Only one spoon of that, young lady, or there won't be enough for my pie!"

Lucy jumped as her mother bustled into the kitchen.

"What have you done with Emily?" remarked Mrs Weaver, busying herself with a rolling pin coated in flour.

Lucy gulped down the sweet nectar before answering. "I'm not sure."

She recounted what had happened in the woods to her bewildered mother.

"She was right beside me..." Lucy dipped the spoon back into the bubbling pot in the hope that her mother was too distracted to notice.

Snatching the spoon out of her daughter's hand, the irate lady snapped, "I suggest that you get back into the wood and find her. Poor girl is obviously lost. She'll be very scared."

Chapter 6

Solomon smiled as he leaned menacingly close to Emily's face. The bewildered girl began to wince as his sour breath surrounded her.

"We can help each other, you know," he sneered.

What on earth do these people eat? Emily mused, as for the second time she was encased in a pungent aroma.

As he settled back into his seat, a large belch filled the air. Emily felt her eyes start to water as the odious gas hit her face.

"I'll begin at the beginning…" His voice began to soften, as he embarked on his tale. "Many moons ago, before you humans lived anywhere near our wood, this all belonged to us." Spreading his hands wide and glaring up to the craggy ceiling, he let out a long, painful sigh. "We played without fear, all day and most of the night. Food was aplenty. We shared this beautiful space with the creatures of the wood, who have made the wise decision to go before being snared by that evil intruder and his gun."

On reflection, Emily couldn't recall seeing any animals as she had wandered through the wood. At home, a woodland walk would've resulted in seeing squirrels, birds and the occasional fox. She found herself starting to feel quite sorry for the strange little man. Then she remembered…

"I saw how you behaved in Lucy's garden. Behaving like that won't make people want to help you!" she exclaimed.

The anger was clearly reflected in his voice. "That land belonged to us first!"

Realising that to argue with him would be a very bad idea, Emily readjusted her sitting position (she was sure those ants were nibbling the back of her legs) ready to listen to the rest of his tale.

"Dig, dig, dig. Build, build, build. Noise, noise, noise. It went on and on. Chop, chop, chop. Our trees toppled. Our homes destroyed."

Just as the sorrow Emily had felt for Solomon started to reappear, she noticed the mischievous glint in his eye. With a huge guffaw, he recounted the time that a group of them had spent the night filling in the foundation holes that had been dug throughout that day. As he laughed, he rocked and his beard began to quiver. A cascade of black flies emerged from the ginger mass. Within seconds, Emily's face was covered. She began spitting out the alien invaders as they found their way into her mouth. She screwed up her eyes, protecting them from the onslaught.

Oblivious to Emily's distress, as her arms were flailing around her face, Solomon carried on with his sorry tale.

"So it went on. As the local men dug and built during the day, we rampaged and ruined during the night. Until one morning, after a rather successful night of sabotage, in they came marching, with their shiny guns slung over their shoulders. The rumpus went on for hours. Families were running this way and that, trying not to lose each other. Gun shots filled the air as angry men swarmed through the wood... It was a sorry sight."

His head dropped as Emily swatted the last fly away from her nose. A large tear dropped onto the mat below and a little sob escaped from the poor grubbler's mouth.

"Wh...what happened next?" ventured Emily.

The sombre silence was broken by Simpkins, who literally rolled into the room. "We signed a pact. A pact that meant we could stay here, in the woods, but that they had the right to build on and hunt in these parts... Sad times, Miss Emily... Sad times."

Solomon's head slowly rose from its melancholy daze. "We had no choice – no guns for us or fancy work tools. We was defeated."

"This is all very sad," said Emily. "But I don't see how I can help."

Simpkins started to clear his throat in a very loud manner. Emily stared in his direction as Solomon glared at him.

"Errrr, just thought you ought to know, Mr Solomon, sir, that the other girl is currently roaming through the woods, sir. My guess is that she be looking for her mate."

Throwing his hands towards the ceiling, the older grubbler shook his head. "That's what you think, is it?" came the sarcastic reply.

Swinging a stick through the hedgerow, Lucy was feeling fed up. The late afternoon sky was starting to take on the bleak shadow of evening and there had been no sign of Emily. With a sigh, the young girl flopped to the ground, lying back onto the leafy blanket that covered the woodland floor. She wanted to rest...just for a minute or two...

She was woken by a sharp prod to her side. Ouch! A pair of green eyes as big as saucers were fixed on her.

"You need to come with me!" His rancid breath made her wince.

"I don't think so!" she retorted, feeling just a little bit scared and confused.

With a stomp of his foot, the ground below her began to shake. Like a spider retrieving its prey from the web, the mossy ground began to swallow her. Lucy's screams echoed around the underground cavern as she fell, landing in a crumpled heap at the foot of the elder grubbler.

Solomon leant over her, his beard tickling her arm. As she moved her head away from his overpowering breath, she noticed a chubby little caterpillar force its way through his tangled beard, followed by another and another.

"Hi," came a voice from the corner of the cramped little room.

Moving her attention away from the fascinating little creatures, Lucy looked over towards the voice and felt a sense of relief wash over her as she recognised Emily's dulcet tones.

Solomon leaned forwards, his grinning face visible to both girls. They watched in horror as a thick black tongue pushed crooked yellowing teeth backwards and forwards like pillowcases flapping in the wind. Rubbing chubby, sweaty hands together, Solomon sat back, whistling loudly through the gaps in his teeth.

"I have a little job for you girlies," he announced.

Tentatively, Emily moved nearer to her friend, yet taking care to keep the required distance away. Lucy started to shuffle in Emily's direction, but the prickly stares from the anxious girl made Lucy stop in her tracks. With their attention clearly focused on the gruesome little man, he began his explanation.

"I had this cunning little plan, so I did. Biggest mistake I made was relying too much on 'im!" At this point, Solomon waved his hat in the direction of Simpkins, who was aimlessly picking at his fingernails with a piece of rather rusty-looking metal.

As he waved his hat, the girls noticed a tiny blue butterfly make its escape from the dark cavern that encased Solomon's head and disappear, as if by magic, through the wooden grooves of the walls. It was quite fascinating, the number of creatures that had chosen to live in close quarters with such a grubby individual!

"My plan, oh yes, my plan! It was a good'un. When I comes up with a plan, tis always a good'un." Moving his face even closer to the girls, he made them recoil as his rancid breath sprayed over them. "Yup, when I has a plan..."

Emily's heart was thudding. Not only was

she in very close quarters to this odious little man but he had breathed on her too. Goodness knows what germs or bugs had been spirited in her direction. Trying to disguise her discomfort, and with tears pricking her eyes, she asked him about his plan and how he expected the girls to help.

With a sniff and a wipe of his nose on his threadbare sleeve, he began. "Me plan was to use your little Ada. A star that girl, always has time for us." Nodding in Lucy's direction he carried on. "She used to sneak out some of your ma's fruit cake and helped me wife with the little'uns when they got too much of a handful. What a treasure!"

At the mention of fruit cake, the girls noticed him rummage around in his trouser pocket and produce what looked like a small cowpat but was in fact a rather squashed piece of Ma's fruit cake. Beaming as he ate, and with another noisy sniff, he carried on with his story.

"Me plan was to use young Ada as bait."

As he spoke, crumbs of cake spurted out of his hanging mouth, hitting the willow beneath them. Excited ants scurried out of every nook and cranny in hopes of retrieving a tasty morsel. Squirming at the sight, Emily wished he would just get on with telling them what he wanted them to do.

Sensing her discomfort, he grinned and continued. "Was going to use young Ada as bait to entice that snooty daughter of theirs into our realm. Then, well, then...'old her 'ostage!"

"He means Clara." Lucy leaned in towards Emily. "She's the daughter of the people who live in the big house, Mr and Mrs White."

Emily shuffled backwards. Surely Lucy realised by now the unease she felt at being close to others.

"Yup, 'old her 'ostage until they gave up any rights to these woods. These woods be our woods and we want 'em back!" The anger welling up inside Solomon exploded, as he thumped the floor with clenched fists, scattering groups of tiny insects to every corner of the room.

"I can see ya, trying to wheedle your way out of the room!"

Following the grubbler's gaze, the girls just caught a glimpse of Simpkins' coattails as he disappeared through the ramshackle doorway.

"It was all his fault... Lost her he did..." As he shook with anger, an explosion erupted that sent what was left of the colony of insects crowded beneath them flying upwards like a shower of confetti.

"Lost who?" the girls chorused, as they gulped for air amidst the stench that surrounded them.

Chapter 7

She often sat behind the curtain, sometimes venturing over to the bed when safe in the knowledge that the occupant was fast asleep. It was often a restless sleep, but sleep just the same. On this particular day, she had sensed someone following her as she skipped through the wood, yet whenever she turned to face her stalker no one was there. Finding the portal was never easy, but she always managed. Careful footing took her over the stream to the gnarled old oak tree with knots like blemishes and an earthy smell, which Ada embraced with a deep breath in. Standing on her tiptoes she could just reach the piece of old, wizened bark protruding from the third knot down below the lowest branch. As she pressed her palm against the rough wood, the crisp carpet of leaves beneath her feet disappeared to be replaced with a flight of cold stone steps. As she mounted the steps, a sense of foreboding filled her body from tip to toe. She looked cautiously around her as she settled behind the curtain to keep watch over her charge.

Within minutes, she felt a presence. An uncomfortable smell surrounded her and then a feeling of nothingness…

It took a while for her eyes to adjust in the darkness that engulfed her. Feeling rather giddy and unsteady on her feet, Ada stumbled forwards. All she could recall was the smell. She had encountered that aroma before but couldn't quite remember where. On unsteady feet, she cautiously moved on through what looked like a long eerie tunnel. It was dark and endless, like an encroaching thundercloud. Her heart was a drum beating a fast rhythm against the wall of her chest. Steadying herself, she grabbed the walls of the tunnel. Compacted soil covered her shaking hands. "I'm underground!" she blurted out.

"Hello… Hello… Is there someone there?"

Not expecting any sort of reply, Ada stopped. Her heart was now racing as if it was against the clock. She froze.

"Hello…" It was a girl's voice; Ada was sure of that.

Just as she turned to flee, an outstretched hand grabbed her arm. The resounding scream that followed seemed to bounce off every fleck of dust and every particle of mud that held the tunnel together.

Yawning, arms stretched upwards, Simpkins woke up from his slumber. What was that noise? Puzzling sound, he thought to himself. A bit like a startled cat. Distracting him from these thoughts, a gurgling sensation rose from the pit of his stomach. Travelling at speed, it seemed to explode into the air like a starting pistol. Thinking about the rather delicious slab of fruit cake that was lurking in his cupboard at home (safely snaffled from Lucy's kitchen when her mother had been occupied with the antics of other such devious grubblers) he suddenly realised she had gone!

A sense of panic overtook him. Where could she be?

"He's going to do for me. He really is." These words were being uttered at regular intervals.

Spinning around on the spot, trying to decide in which direction his charge might have gone, Simpkins became quite dizzy and collapsed in a heap.

"He's gonna do for me. He really is!" His sobs could be heard echoing down the now empty chamber.

As Clara and Ada emerged from the mouth of the tunnel, Ada embraced the freshness of the night air whilst admiring the luminous gleam of the full moon. With her eyes now accustomed to the moonlight, she realised she was in the garden of what was a very impressive house. Both girls dropped down onto the damp grass beneath an old elm tree.

Clara smiled at Ada. "I do hope that we can be friends. I don't have friends." Her smile started to falter.

"What were you doing in the tunnel?" Ada didn't feel afraid, which surprised her in the circumstances.

"Escaping…" came the reply.

Taking her time, Ada looked at the face of the girl sitting beside her. Empty eyes showed no happiness as she purposefully picked at the grass around her.

"Escaping? Escaping from who?"

"Escaping from *what* should be the question." Clara tilted her head towards the house, which on closer examination Ada decided was quite bleak and actually not that welcoming. "My family aren't the nicest people and the only chance I get for some freedom and peace to be myself is at night in this garden amongst the stars and any night-time visitors."

No sooner had she uttered these words than the still of the night was interrupted by the cry of an owl as it landed softly on the branches above them.

By the light of the moon, Ada could see wild rabbits scurrying in and out of the overgrown entrance to the tunnel from which the girls had just emerged.

Clara smiled. "Funny little things, aren't they, rushing here, rushing there, nibbling at anything worth eating as they go. If I sit very still and quiet, just there," she pointed to a low stone wall, which gradually disappeared amongst the thicket of leaves, "they will come close and let me stroke them."

The girls sat for a moment, both lost in their own thoughts, when Ada began to shiver. Ever observant, Clara nudged her new-found friend and suggested they went inside.

Carefully, Clara pushed the old, heavy door open. Ada cautiously followed her into a small narrow corridor. Clara closed the door and gently pushed down the latch. With a whisper to her voice, she instructed Ada to tiptoe quietly along the wooden floor. The narrow corridor suddenly opened into an impressive hallway. Even in the dark, Ada could tell that Clara lived in a comfortable home. As they reached the staircase, which spiralled gently upwards,

Clara guided her nervous companion to avoid the creakiest of steps. Eventually, they reached the door to Clara's bedroom. Warily turning the handle, she let them both in and only seemed to relax once the door was shut quietly behind them. Indicating to Ada to sit on the bed, she lit the gas lamp, which illuminated the room.

Ada scanned the room, taking in her lavish surroundings. Used to sharing a small, cramped bed with her cousin she was impressed with the large, comfortable bed that she found herself sitting on. Running her fingers over the pink, paisley eiderdown, she felt the stirrings of envy creep over her. It wasn't a feeling she felt comfortable with, but what else could she feel when comparing Clara's bedroom to her own small, drab shared space. Slipping off her shoes, Ada was comforted by the softness beneath her feet. The coarse feel of Lucy's bedroom floor was no comparison.

Turning the key in the lock, Clara yawned. "Let's get some sleep."

Swinging her legs up onto the bed, Clara felt her body sink into the comforting softness beneath her. Eyelids closed like shutters and she fell into a deep sleep.

Ada on the other hand was feeling quite anxious. As much as she enjoyed adventures now was the time to go home yet she sensed that Clara would be reluctant to agree to that. Anyway, she didn't know how to get home!

Despite the cosiness of the bed and the wave of tiredness which swept over her, Ada couldn't sleep. A familiar dampness found itself in the corner of her eyes and a lonely sadness crept over her. Thoughts of her parents would settle her she was sure of that. She often imagined what they would look like now rather than the grainy snapshots of how they looked before they left her. Comforting images began to move through her mind, as she dozed on and off throughout the night.

As Ada struggled with sleep, a hapless Simpkins was experiencing a struggle of his own. With eyes tightly shut and hands over his ears, he could only imagine the mayhem raging around him. Clumps of hardened soil rained down on him like violent hailstones as the wild boar stomped around the room lashing out at anything in his path.

Falling forwards, as the force of Solomon's kick caught his backside, Simpkins' face hit the floor. Spitting out the rancid moss that had polluted his mouth, Simpkins looked up at the furious grubbler. "Sorry..." he spluttered.

Tension filled the room. Solomon's cheeks were red and his heart was racing. With clenched jaw and dry mouth, he couldn't respond.

Looking daggers towards the quaking Simpkins, he dropped down onto his gnarled throne.

"Cake?" A shaking hand offered the last crumbling morsel.

Never able to refuse such a treat, Solomon grabbed at it with both hands. They sat together, one munching noisily, the other watching cautiously, too scared to move. The sweet, sugary treat seemed to mellow the angry little man, as a huge crumb-filled smile spread across his face. "I have a plan…"

Chapter 8

"Lost who?" the girls repeated with more urgency.

"Who? Who do ya think?" With a huge yawn that was followed by a disgusting belch, the grubbler continued. "Ada."

"We think we know where she…"

Lucy glared in Emily's direction in an effort to silence her friend.

"Where she what?" The craggy face pushed its way into Emily's personal space.

Reeling backwards, the startled girl stammered, "We found her hankie in the wood… so…she may have been wandering there?"

Emily wasn't too sure that this sounded very convincing. However, it wasn't that far from the truth.

"Mmm…that's as may be, but I think we'll start where *that* buffoon lost her."

Jabbing a hairy, slightly bent finger in their direction, he beckoned the two girls to follow him. As he pushed hard against the coarse, bumpy wall, an opening appeared and the girls dutifully followed him into a narrow, dark, stifling tunnel.

They jumped as the grumpy voice bellowed, "Come out, come out wherever you are, you sniffling little creep!"

Within seconds, the small group was joined by a very sheepish Simpkins who skulked behind them.

"Get up here with me!"

Dutifully, the quaking grubbler joined his leader. "Now these two reckon she's in the wood somewhere. Found her hankie they say. What do you say?"

"Definitely lost her in the tunnel, sir. Definitely did!"

With a deep sigh, the elder grubbler pushed on through the tunnel with Simpkins hurrying to keep up. The girls followed, Lucy first with Emily following a safe distance behind.

The grim passageway seemed to be never-ending. Occasionally another underpass would appear to the side and Emily could tell from Simpkins' worried expression and dithering manner that he wasn't too sure whether to veer off down one of these boltholes or stay on the main track.

On they trudged. Every now and then, Solomon would start to whistle a rather merry tune and add a bounce to his step. However, within minutes the whistling would stop and the pace would quicken as he marched along grumbling under his breath.

Just as the girls were starting to feel tired and thirsty, Emily caught a glimpse of sunlight bouncing off the uneven tunnel wall.

"We might want to make our way towards the light," Emily ventured.

Stopping in their tracks, both grubblers turned and stared at the girls...

"Exactly what I was thinking." Wanting to redeem himself in front of the elder grubbler, Simpkins was nodding in agreement with Emily's suggestion.

The strange little band carried on, following the source of the light. After what seemed like an eternity, with tired feet and a raging thirst, they reached the mouth of the tunnel. The entrance, covered in tangled branches with a floor of damp, muddy leaves, opened to a vast well-kept garden. Scanning her surroundings, Emily soon caught sight of a water butt over on the far side of the garden. The four companions clearly had the same idea; resting weary feet and quenching thirst was a top priority. But how to cross the garden without being seen?

Cautiously, Lucy nudged Emily with her elbow. She knew the little girl didn't like being touched, yet she could think of no other way to get her attention. She nodded her head towards a patch of long, unkempt grassland, which on closer inspection housed two tatty yet well-loved, large flowerpots. With a whisper she smiled, "Shame we aren't small enough to fit under those!"

"What's the plan then?" asked an inquisitive Simpkins, whilst closely scrutinising something he had just pulled from his nose.

Watching him roll whatever it was into a small ball and then flick it ceremoniously into the air made Emily feel quite sick. Lucy nudged her again. Emily was starting to feel more relaxed about her friend being close to her.

"What are we going to do?"

Years of experience had taught Solomon to be alert in unfamiliar situations and he noticed the furtive glances between the girls. Sidling up to Lucy, he whispered, "If you 'as an idea, little missy, share it!"

Sighing, Lucy explained her thoughts. "We need a drink. We need to rest and think about what to do next. If we can get over to that water butt, we can drink then rest in the long grass behind it. But we need to get there, unseen."

Tipping back his head and releasing a raucous roar he laughed, "Looking at them there pots weren't ya?"

With a pull on his beard, a twitch of his nose and a click of his chubby fingers Emily felt a dizziness she had never felt before. Tinkling sensations ran from her head to her toes. Within seconds Emily was no taller than Solomon himself.

Chapter 9

When Ada woke from her restless sleep, Clara was already sitting bolt upright in bed waiting impatiently to discuss her plans for the day. Nobody must find out that Ada was there. Clara was sure that her parents wouldn't approve, and she couldn't risk them finding out about her late-night jaunts into the garden. Clara had told Ada that her nightly encounters were all she had in her life to look forward to. Ada decided that this was an extremely sad situation to be in. Although Clara's bedroom was more luxurious than Ada could ever imagine and her garden was a heavenly sanctuary, Ada still preferred the cosy, warm atmosphere of her aunt's shabby cottage.

Tummy rumbling, Ada was aware that she hadn't eaten since yesterday lunchtime, the lack of food adding to her low spirits.

"What are you looking for?" yawned Ada.

"Something to smuggle you some food in. There must be something somewhere."

"You could use this," Ada replied with a growling stomach, handing over her hankie. "It's clean. I would like some food. I'm very hungry."

Watching Clara get dressed, Ada marvelled at the careful way she folded her nightclothes and climbed into a pretty, high-necked dress, which puffed at the sleeves. She had never owned such an attractive outfit. She and Lucy shared clothes and she smiled to herself recalling the rush every morning to get to the best outfit for the day.

Tying her long blonde hair back into a neat bow, Clara told Ada to curl up under the bed if she feared anyone might come into the room. Although Clara would lock the door behind her, she warned Ada that her mother held the master key and could appear at any time. As Clara left the room, Ada thought to herself how sad it was that someone who had all these wonderful things around her seemed so unhappy.

There was never much conversation at the breakfast table. Clara's parents passed the usual polite comments to each other whilst barely noticing their daughter. This always made Clara feel quite empty and sad, but not today. She was anxious to just eat and disappear back to the sanctuary of her bedroom. As the kitchen maid placed the platters of food onto the table, Clara marvelled at her parents' rudeness. Not once did they acknowledge the young woman's presence. Her father had his eyes glued to the morning paper, whilst her mother talked at him about the shortcomings of the new gardener. Clara smiled politely at the maid as she returned to her kitchen duties. Scanning the table, she decided what food would be the easiest to smuggle upstairs. On serving herself the fluffiest of scrambled eggs, she discreetly started to pull the hidden hankie from the sleeve of her dress. But wait! Nothing was there... Probing fingers ran around her wrist and up her sleeve, yet they found nothing. With a sudden loss of appetite, she announced to her parents that she wasn't feeling too well and would go back to bed. Without even a cursory glance in her direction, they carried on with their morning ritual.

As Clara left the dining room, the maid sidled up beside her, pushing a snack tin into her hands. Puzzled, Clara looked up at her.

"This is just in case you get hungry later," said the maid.

"It's very heavy," remarked the grateful girl.

"Well, there's enough to share!" The maid winked at her before returning to the kitchen.

Crossing the hallway, Clara caught sight

of her father's gamekeeper, Mr Fincher. What was he picking up from the bottom of the stairs? Whatever it was, he pushed it into his pocket and gave her a nod of his head as he passed by. Tucking the tin of food under her arm whilst grabbing hold of the handrail, Clara made her careful way up the staircase.

Both girls sat on the plush rug at the end of Clara's bed as they tucked into the breakfast treats. Ada was starting to feel the tiredness lift as the food hit her empty stomach. Suddenly, a knock at the door! With a hint of panic in her eyes, Clara nodded towards the bed. Dutifully, Ada crawled underneath. Ada had often dived under Lucy's bed in search of lost shoes or discarded hair ribbons to be met with piles of dust or fluff, which invaded her nose causing quite a fit of the sneezes. It was always her that did those things. Lucy lost things; Ada found them. She always felt the need to help people, to please people, even those ridiculous, annoying little men from the wood.

Showing a confidence she really did not feel, Clara opened the bedroom door. The kitchen maid stood in front of her.

"Thought you might get thirsty," she said, pushing a jug of cooled milk and two glasses into Clara's hands. With a knowing smile, she turned and made her way back to the kitchen.

Pushing her face under the bed, Clara announced, "She knows!"

Over the next few days, life fell into a pattern for Ada. Stuck in Clara's bedroom during the day, she would dart under the bed when the maid came to clean, which seemed a pointless exercise as the maid clearly knew she was there! She would greedily tuck into the food and drink left behind when the maid had finished her daily chores, but she was starting to get a little bored. At night, she had the chance to use the bathroom and enjoy the splendours of the midnight garden. Clara appeared so serene and content with the situation and became quite prickly towards Ada when she asked about going home.

"They will come looking for me." Ada was picking at the grass around the old elm tree.

The moon was bright that night and the look on Clara's illuminated face told Ada that she had no wish to listen. Ada felt sorry for her young companion but was starting to feel like a caged bird desperate to spread her wings and fly.

"You could come with me," she suggested.

At this, Clara sighed, nodding towards the house. Both girls headed silently back to Clara's room. Lying restless beside her new-found friend that night, Ada was not sure how she was going to find a way out of this unhappy situation she found herself in.

The following day Clara had to go out with her parents, leaving Ada locked in. The day dragged on. Sitting in the window seat, head in hands, hoping that someone might see her, Ada's thoughts wandered. She was missing Lucy and worrying about Emily...

It was strange how she had been drawn to that tree. She had always felt at peace sitting beneath it reading a book or playing with Solomon's children. Nobody else seemed to like the strange little people, but she felt sorry for them. It couldn't have been easy having your home and your community ravaged and ruined. One day, as she sat beneath the old oak tree, listening to the wind whistling through the wood, she heard it.

A cry.

A sob.

The sound of sadness.

It sounded like it was coming from the very soul of the ageing tree. Running her hands up and down the coarse lines of the bark, pushing her ear against every wrinkle, she found it by the third knot down below the lowest branch...

What was that? Ada rubbed her eyes. There it goes again – it's definitely moving!

Chapter 10

The invasion of her personal space was making Emily feel rather uncomfortable. She was squashed together with Solomon under the flowerpot. Pockets of light were visible through the hole in the top of the pot and the many cracks that adorned its sides. Desperately trying not to draw breath too often, Emily worked with the wily little grubbler to move the pot across the garden.

Both girls had spent some time working out a route that would make them less conspicuous to anyone in the house. No help was offered by the two little men who both curled up in the long grass and slept, oblivious to all the creepy crawlies determined to make these grubby creatures their home.

When the route had finally been agreed and the grubblers woken, off they went. Emily was a little annoyed that Lucy had paired up with

Simpkins, who was quite clueless about most things and would follow Lucy's instructions to the letter. She, on the other hand, had Solomon, who, refreshed from his nap, was becoming increasingly annoying.

They stopped midway and Emily tried to grab a breath. Solomon had produced yet another foul smell, which he celebrated with great hilarity. As she turned her face to the top of the pot, she saw it – a silvery wet trail that led from a meandering chink.

She followed the trail from the side of the pot to the top of Solomon's hat and down the side of his face. Nestled by the corner of his mouth was a fat, black slug, its antennae grappling with the sticky strands of the grubbler's beard.

"'Ere, are we moving on again then?"

The sound of his agitated voice brought Emily back to the job in hand.

"Yes… Together… *Now*!"

They moved in unison. It was an odd sight, the girl crawling on her knees and the little man slightly hunched, both pressing against the sides of the ageing pot.

Fiddling with the window sash, Ada finally

managed to push the pane up. Leaning out as far as she dared, her eyes became transfixed by the tatty, old flowerpot. It was… It was moving!

Shifting her body slightly, Ada could just see the far side of the water butt and was mesmerised as she watched a flustered little person emerge from under the pot and tumble across the grass. By the time Emily hit the water butt she was back to her normal size, possibly even taller.

Surely it can't be…but my goodness that girl looks just like Emily. Ada was very confused.

Sliding down from the window and collapsing in complete bewilderment on the floor, Ada knew that if in fact that was Emily she had just seen, then she had to find a way of letting her know she was there.

On reaching the water butt, Emily found Simpkins and Lucy had already quenched their thirst and were sitting waiting, partially hidden by the long grass.

"I'm sure I saw someone at the window," Emily stated as she crawled through the long grass towards her friend.

The girls slithered to a position where they could see the window. It was definitely open but there was no sign of anyone. Distracted by the sound of Solomon slurping from the rusting tap beneath the water butt, Lucy marvelled at the strange little man as he lay, head resting on his hands, beard spread out like a ginger blanket and feet tapping in time to the droplets of rainwater hitting his mouth.

Emily was more distracted by the open window. She felt a very strange sensation. She had felt it before, the day she had spotted Lucy beneath the tree outside of her house. Eyes glued to the window, she was waiting, waiting for something, but she wasn't sure what.

Inside the bedroom, Ada was frantically trying to think of a way to attract attention. Her eyes fell upon a shelf of books above the fireplace. Feeling drawn to the books, she lifted one down and began to flick through the pages. Ada didn't really like school; she found the teachers harsh and unkind. She would rather stay at home and help her aunt clean and keep those pesky grubblers under control. This meant her reading and writing skills were poor. Flicking through the book, all the words seemed to blur into one. Wait…until…nightfall… These words she could read; they jumped out of the page at her. It was a strange sensation, recognising three words out of the jumble of others. Grabbing a piece of coal from the fire grate, she underlined the three words, turned down the corner of the page, then, returning to the open window, she threw the book with all her might in the direction of the water butt and Emily. Watching the book make its descent to the ground, Ada prayed that none of the servants would see it as it passed by the kitchen window.

Lying quietly, looking up at the darkening sky and enjoying the solitude, Simpkins squealed as something hard hit him full in the face. On hearing the noise both girls rushed to his side. Solomon on the other hand just carried on, slurp, slurp, slurp, tap, tap, tap.

"It's a book!" Lucy exclaimed.

Simpkins was rubbing his throbbing nose as Emily wiped away the tears from his eyes with the edge of her sleeve. Meanwhile Lucy was glancing all around her trying to see where the book had come from. Then she too spotted the figure at the window. She could tell it was a girl. As the evening was drawing closer, lights were starting to appear in the kitchen and drawing room. It would be too risky to move closer. However, she wanted to see who the figure at the window was.

Making good use of the fading light, the girls carefully turned the pages hoping to find any clues as to why it had appeared. Emily felt quite at ease and relaxed sitting next to Lucy. She had grown very fond of her new-found friend and this fuelled her hope that when she finally got back home, the pandemic would be over and she once again could embrace those she cared about.

As she reached the page with the turned-down corner, she felt a surge of excitement. There they were, three smudged words… Wait… Until… Nightfall.

Chapter 11

Clara slumped onto the bed. "It's so boring visiting my aunt." Her eyes were fixed on the newly laid fireplace.

Please don't look up at the bookshelf, please don't! These words swam around Ada's head as she tried to be sympathetic.

"It'll be dark soon. We can go out then. Well, when everyone is in bed, obviously!" Ada was starting to feel really quite nervous.

"I don't know. I'm really tired tonight." Clara was yawning as she spoke.

Nerves turned into panic. Panic turned into anger. "You can be really selfish, Clara. Do you realise that?"

Smoothing down her pretty pink dress Clara glared at Ada.

"You keep me locked in this room all day, sometimes on my own. People will be looking for me and when they find me don't you think it will be better if I say I was happy to stay rather than saying I was kept a prisoner?" Tears of frustration were starting to prick at Ada's eyes.

A stony silence followed, which was eventually shattered by the cascade of tears tumbling down Clara's face.

"I just want to go out into the garden later. I want a change from these four walls." Ada's voiced had softened. She knew deep down that the true prisoner here was in fact Clara.

As the tension was growing upstairs, tension downstairs was escalating too. Albert, the family gardener, was sitting at the newly scrubbed kitchen table mystified as to how the old flowerpots he had collected as rubbish had now made their way to the other side of the garden. Rose, the family cook, was flapping around the kitchen, rummaging through the larder looking for something to put together for supper. She had been told that the family were eating out today but they had returned early demanding to be fed. Rose simply couldn't understand why the larder was so low on stock; she was usually so scrupulous with her ordering. Sarah, the friendly kitchen maid, stayed quiet, just watching the drama unfold.

Fincher stood, hands in pockets, leaning against the kitchen door. He was a tall, imposing man, an excellent shot with a rifle. Watching Sarah very closely, he ran his fingers over the neatly embroidered 'A' in the corner of the white hankie that lay crumpled up in his pocket. Not a lot escaped his notice; it was his job to be curious and observant. The fact that the young mistress of the house had spent a lot of time in her bedroom over the last few days and that Sarah had been delivering food to her on a regular basis was suspicious. He was determined to get to the bottom of what was going on.

There was also tension in the garden. The night was drawing in and the moonlight was diluted by the murky autumnal clouds, making it difficult for the girls to see. Any light from the house was gradually blocked as curtain after curtain closed against the dark. What did 'wait until nightfall' mean? How long would they have to wait? Why were they waiting? These questions rattled through Emily's mind unanswered. Lucy was starting to feel uncomfortable. The grass was damp and the grubblers were annoying her. Simpkins would rummage through the long grass, munching on anything he could find there, then cartwheel around the water butt, repeating the process time and time again. Solomon lay in the grass tapping his foot incessantly whilst blowing saliva bubbles from his mouth and getting quite excited when he managed a large one. Emily just sat, staring at the house. What was she thinking about? As Lucy watched, the darkness became more intense and Emily's form started to blend in. Fear gripped Lucy as she moved closer to her friend needing the comfort of her presence.

Fincher was up late, hunched over his ledgers, squinting under the oil lamp. He was sure those grubblers were poaching more than the master thought they were. Fincher and his men would leave traps littering the master's fields but those pesky little blighters never found their way into them. The trouble was, the master didn't quite understand how much money this was losing them. Even a single unskinned rabbit could get a fair price at the local market.

What was that noise? Excellent hearing was an important attribute for a gamekeeper and his was better than most. It had come from the direction of the staircase. Fincher's room was beside the kitchen, which suited him very well. Snacks raided from the cook's larder were a welcome distraction when he was poring over the books. Both his room and the kitchen backed onto the staircase. He was convinced something was going on with the young Miss Clara and he was determined to find out what...

Both girls stood, frozen against the banister. In her desperation to get out Ada had quite forgotten about the creaky stairs. They held their breath as the sinister shadow walked to the bottom of the staircase and stood for a few seconds.

By the time Fincher had returned with his oil lamp both girls had made their way out of the side door and into the garden.

With barely any moonlight streaming through the thick blanket of cloud, the girls instinctively found their way to the old elm tree. Glancing around her, Ada was filled with hope that Emily would find them before the cold night air enticed Clara back to her bedroom. However, it wasn't the nip in the air that bothered Clara. Her leg was aching after a long day out with her parents, who didn't seem to care about her discomfort. She was trying to understand how Ada was feeling but it was difficult; she had never had a friend before.

As Ada scanned the garden, squinting through the dark, she saw it, a sparkle of fireflies circling around the water butt. In amongst the glowing creatures, she noticed two luminous green balls spliced by a yellow flash. As her eyes gradually got accustomed to the dark, she recognised him – the hapless grubbler!

Chapter 12

Grabbing a bemused Clara by the arm, Ada guided her towards the water butt. Suddenly, out of nowhere, both girls were scooped up. With fear rushing through her very core, Ada kicked and struggled against the iron grip that held her. With long strides, Fincher was making his way towards the house, a captured child under each arm.

"Ouch!" He felt a searing pain of sharp teeth puncturing deep into his arm and with a yelp he dropped her…

Running like the wind she made it to the water butt, slicing through the fireflies and collapsing in dew-soaked grass.

"Well, hello!"

With her heart still pounding against her chest, she turned towards the voice.

There he was, Solomon. She had never been so pleased to see someone. He leant towards her, saliva dribbling down into his matted beard, making it glisten against the glow of the lightning bugs.

"Where's your little friend then?" he enquired, whilst drumming his chubby fingers against the side of the water butt.

Shivering in her now damp dress, Ada sat up. Clara was going to be in so much trouble. A sense of guilt came over her. After all, it was on her insistence that they had come out tonight, even though they knew that they had aroused suspicion. Yet Ada just wanted to get back to her family. Just the thought of them radiated warmth through her, which soon stopped the shivering. Her aunt and uncle had been so kind taking her in, caring for her, loving her. How difficult it must have been for Lucy, suddenly having to share her home, her bedroom and her parents. Ada's thoughts were rudely interrupted by louder, more insistent drumming.

"*Well?*"

"If you mean Clara, I'm not sure. What are you doing here anyway? Have you come to rescue me? Was that Emily I spotted earlier? How do you know Emily? How did you even find Emily? Did you send that grubbler to snatch me?"

"Ughhhhhh… Questions, questions, questions. Boring, boring, boring." Solomon flicked his beard as he spoke and Ada was fascinated by the small black blob trampolining across the ginger mass.

Launching herself out of the darkness, Lucy flung her arms around Ada's neck. Watching this emotional reunion, Emily not only felt relieved but excited. Her heart was thudding against her chest as she approached the embracing girls.

Standing back, Lucy allowed both girls to see each other.

"Hello…" Ada smiled.

"Hi…"

Emily had so many questions she wanted Ada to answer, but it was clear that they needed to move quickly. Questions could wait for later.

"Come on, let's try and find that tunnel…" Turning towards the far side of the garden, Lucy found she couldn't move. Knelt at her feet and with a firm grip on her ankles was Solomon.

"Ain't going anywhere without the other one!" The determination was clear in his eyes.

Meanwhile, there was a huge commotion in the house. A furious Fincher had awoken Rose as he stomped into the kitchen dumping a poor shaking Clara onto a well-worn wooden chair.

"What on earth is going on, Mr Fincher?"

Rose had arrived in the kitchen dressed head to toe in a white crumpled nightie. She was a short woman and the nightgown trailed behind her like a ghost.

"Keep an eye on her whilst I rouse the master!" Fincher barked out his orders.

Clara felt very scared. Her parents would never forgive such insolent behaviour. She curled both legs around the rough chair legs for support as she watched a very flustered Rose tidy an already immaculate kitchen. All the gleaming pans hung on the pan hooks above the stove ordered in size, smallest to largest. The plates on the dresser were neatly stacked, with the jugs and bowls out on the breakfast tray ready for morning. Looking down to the freshly scrubbed floor, Clara wondered if she would ever be allowed out of the house on her own again. As her eye line moved across the gleaming tiles, they met a pair of bare feet poking out from beneath a long, white, baggy nightshirt. Slowly lifting her eyes, Clara encountered Sarah.

With a finger pressed to her lips, Sarah motioned towards the back door and smiled a knowing smile. With a swipe of her hand, Sarah knocked the milk jug from the breakfast tray and Clara watched as it splintered onto the cold, hard floor.

Rose swiped Sarah across the back of the head. "You stupid, careless girl. Quick, quick, get a brush!"

Apologising, as she rubbed the side of her head, Sarah added to the confusion. "Where will

I find a brush? I'm so sorry... Where will I find a brush?"

Pushing past her, mumbling something about stupid, lazy kitchen maids, Rose went off to the broom cupboard. With a wink and a glance from Sarah, Clara knew that this was her chance! Closing the door softly behind her, she was back into the darkness of the midnight garden.

The glint of light from the opening door distracted Solomon and his vice-like grip on Lucy's ankle weakened. Taking the opportunity, Lucy wriggled free.

"Quick, run!" she shouted to the others.

As the girls flew across the garden, they grasped Clara by the arms and she led them to the mouth of the hidden tunnel.

Chapter 13

Once they had scrambled through the brambles, at the tunnel entrance they were encased in darkness. Tension filled the air, as the girls were unsure as to what to do next. The commotion coming from the garden behind them spurred Emily on. Showing a confidence that she didn't actually feel, she ensured Clara was safely squashed in between herself and Ada. Lucy boldly followed at the rear.

"If we keep each other close, we'll be OK," she called along the line of anxious girls.

Moving cautiously through the gloom, they were silent. The only sound to be heard was their feet on the hard, crisp ground, until a chink of light caught them from behind along with the sound of muffled voices. The girls knew that they needed to push on quickly; they were going to be in so much trouble. Passageway after passageway streamed off from the main underpass just like a rabbit warren. Clara felt an incredible sense of responsibility for the others yet she knew that her father would be hot on their trail. She could not even begin to think of the punishments that faced her after such a dramatic escape from home. But deep down she didn't really care. These past few days with Ada had been the most exciting she had ever known.

The voices were getting closer and the light was getting brighter. Clara knew that she was the one slowing the others down. With a sudden surge of energy, she darted to the left down a narrow passage. As she moved, she lost her grip on Emily's hand. This sudden change in direction took Ada by surprise. Losing her footing she stumbled.

The harrowing scream could be heard from every corner of the underground cavern. Tentatively, the remaining girls crawled to the edge of the ravine, three dark heads huddled together looking in horror at Clara hanging from a branch, with her smart dress acting like a parachute.

As they came to a skidding halt behind them, Fincher and Clara's father's fury was clear to see.

"Clara, you foolish girl!"

The power behind the voice echoed around the ravine. The ledge the girls were sitting on began to vibrate causing shards of rock to break away and rain down on the frightened girl beneath them. One piece was larger and heavier than the others. As it crashed below, it hit the very branch Clara was hanging from.

Crack! The branch began to splinter.

The look of fury on Mr White's face had quickly changed to fear. He was frightened for his daughter's safety.

Seemingly out of nowhere, a long, twine-like vine trailed down past the frightened girls' very noses and down, down, down to the crumbling branch. Wiping the tears from her eyes, Emily watched in awe as Simpkins appeared to slide down towards the stricken girl. He managed to tie the vine around her middle just as the branch made its final creak and disappeared into the abyss below. Both Clara and Simpkins were now swinging in a precarious manner to and fro. No one, including Simpkins, knew quite what to do. Fincher and Mr White tried to catch the vine several times as it passed their way but it was just too far for them to reach. The girls stayed huddled together watching in horror as the tie around Clara's waist slowly began to loosen.

With a thudding heart and throbbing head, she was gripping onto the vine. A sense of panic was visible across her face. She could see the girls in the distance; Ada had her eyes covered and Emily was shaking with fear. The tie around her waist was gone; desperately trying to grab Simpkins' foot was too much of a stretch. She was falling. Spiralling downwards. Voices of despair were ringing through her ears.

There was an eerie silence on the ledge above. Tears were streaming from eyes, bodies were trembling and ears were pricked just waiting to hear the terrible thud from below.

Simpkins had been quite forgotten about, swinging aimlessly around in never-decreasing circles. Unbeknownst to them, Clara's fall had been broken by something sticky and very prickly. Too shocked to move she just lay there amidst the smelly, bristly blanket.

"Oi! Get off me beard!"

Chapter 14

Not daring to look downwards, Clara moved to face the strange little man who had just saved her.

"Thank you," was all she could manage to say as she disentangled herself and moved backwards from the edge of the gorge into which she had fallen.

Solomon yawned, then followed through with a loud, smelly belch, which made poor Clara flinch. Grabbing her roughly by the arm, he marched her through the dark, cold maze of tunnels that would eventually bring them back to Clara's garden. Clara was feeling very shaky. Her legs were wobbling as she tried to keep up. How could such a short person achieve such long strides? Using the mud-covered walls to support her she followed in the wake of her determined rescuer.

Dawn was breaking as they emerged from the brambled entrance. The garden was a very sombre stage. Her mother was there, standing in her nightgown sobbing. Rose was fussing around the other girls giving them hot milk and popping shawls around their cold shoulders as they sat huddled together on the doorstep. Fincher and her dad were talking in quiet yet earnest voices. The tense atmosphere was suddenly broken.

"I think a reward is due here. Feel free to thank me." Flicking the side of his hat and smiling that broad devious grin, Solomon addressed the crowd.

Stumbling out of the tunnel behind the odious little man, Clara felt a sense of achievement that far outweighed any reward.

Later that day, the girls were sitting together under the old oak tree. The weather was unusually warm for the time of year and the sun was breaking through the wispy clouds. Rose had found them a large picnic rug and made them some sweet, sugary lemonade, which prickled their tongues as they drank. Lucy's mother had given them a large slab of her celebrated fruit cake, which just melted in their mouths.

Clara had never felt so happy. She had friends at last and her father and Fincher had agreed to allow the grubblers to live undisturbed in the wood for as long as they wished. Emily sensed Solomon wasn't altogether happy with these arrangements but for the time being he seemed content sitting in a nook of the tree, one hand pulling apart a rather large mushroom and the other full of crumbling cake. In between munching mushroom and cake, he would tilt back his head, hat and all, and ferret around in the bramble bushes, grabbing at the blackberries with what were left of his rotting teeth. Any stray crumbs that missed the greedy grubbler's mouth were soon devoured by the inhabitants of his straggly beard.

Ada and Lucy were so happy to be back together just in time to celebrate their birthday.

"I can't believe you share a birthday. How exciting," said Emily.

"Not just a birthday but we were born at roughly the same time, 9.30 in the evening of the 13th of September," replied Lucy as she gave her cousin a hug. "I'm sure that's what makes us so close."

Ada sensed that Emily had something to share but she wasn't about to press her friend about it. As the birthday girls chattered and ate, with Clara soaking up every bit of the conversation, Emily started to think about her own family and wondered where they were and what they were doing. Noticing the faraway look in Emily's eyes, Ada stood up. Reaching up on the very tips of her toes, she managed to find the old, wizened bark protruding from the third knot down below the lowest branch. Pressing her palm against the rough wood, she smiled at Emily. "It's time…"

"It's time you got up, you lazy thing!"

Emily crawled out from beneath her duvet to find her mum sitting on the edge of her bed.

With a sudden rush of affection, Emily flung her arms around her mum's neck.

"Woah! What a lovely surprise," said Mum. "It's been ages since we've had a cuddle!"

"The good news is that the government are saying that things are improving. We can meet up with friends again. In small groups and we need to still be careful, but it's a start to getting back to normal."

A huge smile spread across Emily's face.

"So," continued Mum, "Dad is coming to pick you up and I think he plans on heading towards the safari park! Then I thought maybe Janella could come over for a picnic tea in the garden."

Pulling herself up in her bed, Emily looked around her room. It was just as it always had been, her mountain of cuddly toys teetering on the edge of her bed and the bookcase rammed full of her favourite stories.

Still smiling, she looked towards her mum.

"Mum, what time was I born?"

"That's an odd question!" Emily's mum shrugged, then replied, "9.30, my love, 9.30pm on Sunday the 13th of September."

As Mum got up and left the bedroom, Emily made her way towards the curtains. Slowly opening them she was certain that she spotted two luminous green balls spliced by a yellow flash circling around the window. As she moved closer to the glass pane she saw them, in the corner of the windowsill: a small pile of crumbs, which looked suspiciously like crumbs from a rather delightful fruit cake.